CommBank
MATILDAS

MATILDAS
IT'S DONE

There's a change in the air –
can you feel it?

'Til ~~we play our first international match~~
~~we claim our first trophy~~
~~we qualify for our first World Cup~~
~~we score our first World Cup goal~~
~~they call us the Matildas~~
~~we get a write-up in the papers~~
~~we win our first World Cup match~~
~~we play in Sydney 2000~~
~~the stands start filling up~~
~~we're women's Asian Cup champions~~
~~we get our own jersey~~
~~we score a World Cup hat-trick~~
~~we make the quarter finals~~
~~we outdo ourselves in Tokyo 2020~~
~~they build the Home of the Matildas~~
~~we play a World Cup on home soil~~
~~we make the quarter finals again~~
~~other sports pause and watch us~~
~~we smash a history-making penalty~~
~~we storm into the semis~~
~~the whole country takes notice~~
~~the whole world takes notice~~

More books in partnership with Football Australia

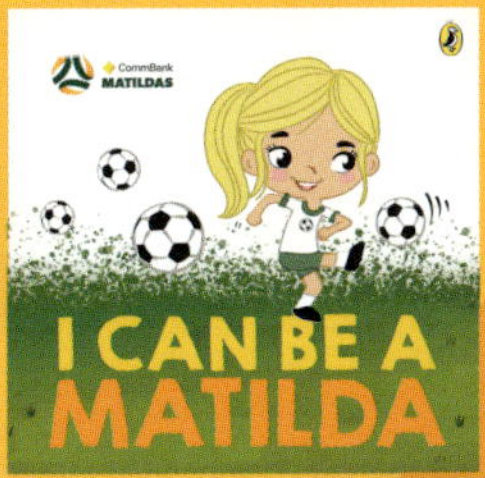

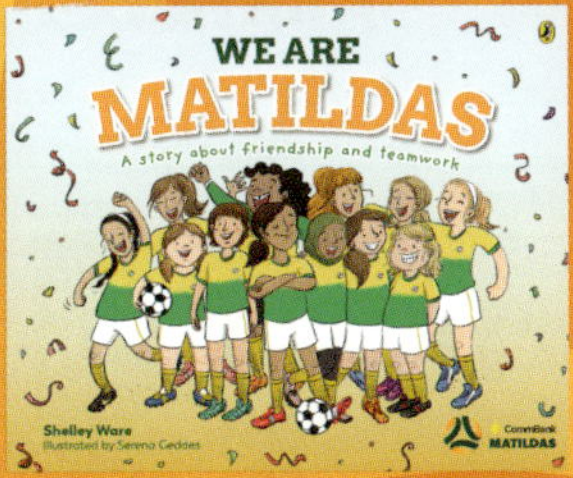

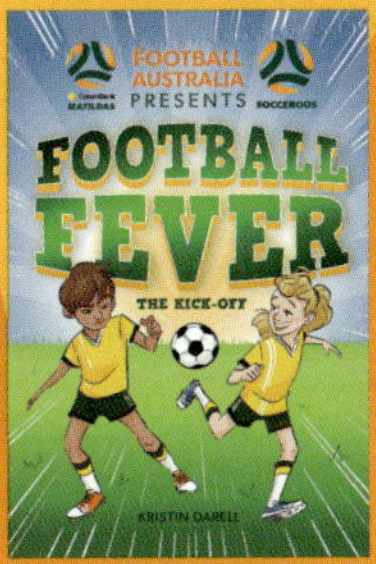

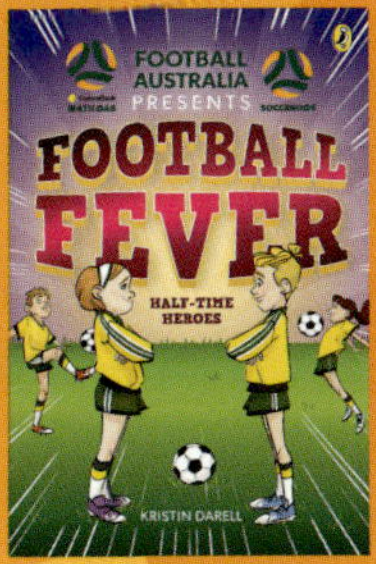

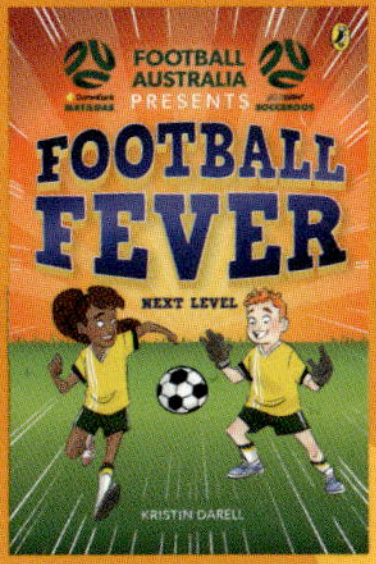

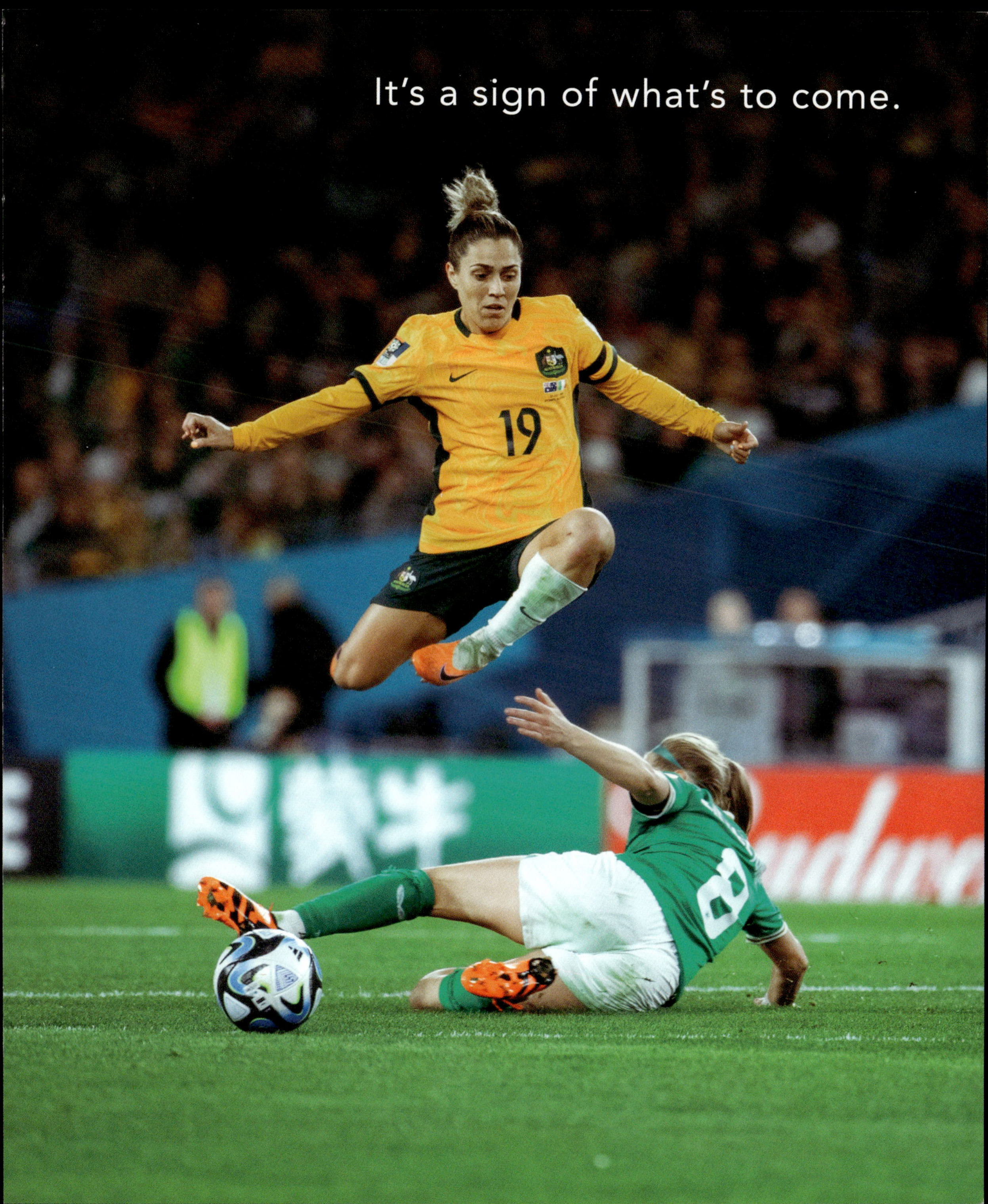
It's a sign of what's to come.

Can you hear that quiet buzz?

Or feel the rising hum?

A ball swishes in the back of the net,

studded boots rip turf as you run

And we hear twenty-three
cries of victory

after another job well done.

FOOTBALL
UNITES
the World
FIFA

while wearing green and gold galore.

We all hold our breath

before erupting in a resounding roar.

We watch you score a World Cup goal

and your second and your third.

We stand behind you and
stomp and cheer

so loud the whole world heard.

Now there's more hard work to do.

The battle's far from won.

But can you see us stand and cheer?

It's a sign of what's to come.

Through every kick, tackle
and goal you save,

the whole nation stops to watch.

We see the skill, the tricks
and form . . .

23

AUS

how every move is just topnotch.

We see you face trials head-on

and take the bad with the good.

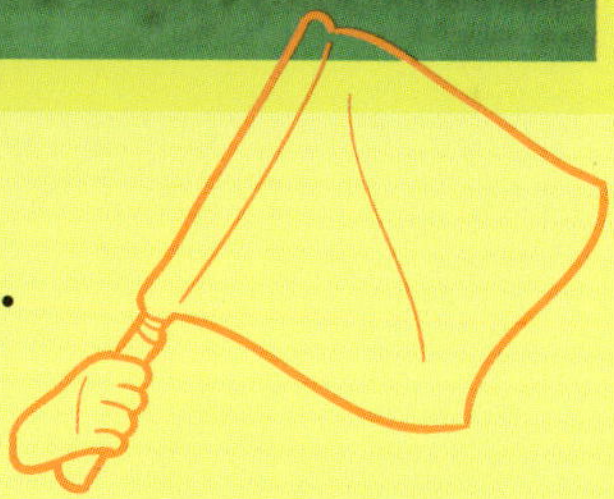

Still, you persist, showing
spirit and grace

and strength in sisterhood.

We beat drums and
call out battle cries.

We're an army of green and gold.

We forget about everything else

as we see history unfold.

We can't stop watching
our TV screens.

We don't want to miss a beat.

We fill up the stands and
show our support.

We’re driven to our feet.

With bated breath and wide eyes,

we watch you fight to stake your claim

On a match that's up for the taking,

but you'll have to
show perfect aim.

Then, after scoring
neck and neck,

it all comes down to this:

WE ARE MATILDAS
NEVER SAY

There's one more shot at
one more win . . .

and, of course, you didn't miss.

The buzz is electric, loud and strong,

and with it comes rolls of thunder,

As millions like us jump
around and scream

for our Matildas from Down Under.

You hold so many hearts aloft

out on the field in full view.

GO TEAM

What we witness truly moves us,
so we send our own hearts to you.

We share in your joy,

see amazing feats . . .

21
AUS

We also feel your pain.

There might not be a trophy this time,

but our faith in you remains.

The ink won't have dried
in the history books

before you start another day.

Another chance to kick some goals

and cross some off along the way.

This journey isn't over.

You fought such a brilliant fight.

And now we're looking to the future,

with your fire that still burns bright.

We saw so many changes –

more signs of what's to come.

There's a longer list of
achievements now,

that you're crossing off one by one.

Think of us, who
watch you play

in every match there is to see.

With soaring hearts, we see in you

the players we want to be.

There's so much to celebrate

and we know you've only just begun.

So, we'll keep cheering for you, Matildas,

and we won't stop . . .

'til it's done.

~~we're all over every front page~~
~~everyone knows our names~~
~~girls dream of being us~~
~~boys are wearing our jerseys~~
~~over 11 million watch us live~~
~~we score an unforgettable goal~~
~~the crowd gets to its feet~~
~~we unite Australia~~
~~women's football gets funded~~
grassroots football gets funded
we bring it at Paris 2024
we go again in 2027
we leave a legacy…

We're not done #tilitsdone

MATILDAS
IT'S DONE

CommBank
MATILDAS

PENGUIN BOOKS

UK | USA | Canada | Ireland | Australia
India | New Zealand | South Africa | China

Penguin Random House Australia

Penguin Random House Australia is part of the Penguin Random House group of companies whose addresses can be found at global.penguinrandomhouse.com.

First published by Penguin Books, an imprint of Penguin Random House Australia Pty Ltd, in 2023

Cover and internal design by Caroline Lee and Rebecca King © Penguin Random House Australia Pty Ltd

Cover photograph © Tiffany Williams/Football Australia.

Internal photographs:
Mary Fowler, Ellie Carpenter and Caitlin Foord: Robert Cianflone/Getty Images Sport; Mackenzie Arnold: Alex Pantling/FIFA; team: Robert Cianflone/Getty Images Sport; Melbourne fans: Asanka Ratnayake/Getty Images Sport; Alanna Kennedy and Stine Ballisager: Cameron Spencer/Getty Images Sport; Sam Kerr and Steph Catley: Brendon Thorne/Getty Images Sport; Sydney fans: Jenny Evans/Getty Images Sport; Cortnee Vine: Justin Setterfield/Getty Images Sport; Cortnee Vine goal: William West/AFP; Matildas players: Quinn Rooney/Getty Images Sport; all other photographs: Tiffany Williams/© Football Australia.

Internal images: © mhatzapa/Shutterstock.com, © Tiwat K/Shutterstock.com, © balabolka/Shutterstock.com, © JosepPerianes/Shutterstock.com, © Dmytro Nychytalyuk/Shutterstock.com, © JJ Chamon/Shutterstock.com, © Prokhorovich/Shutterstock.com, © Kanate/Shutterstock.com, © primiaou/Shutterstock.com, © Rebellion Works/Shutterstock.com

Printed and bound in Australia by Griffin Press

NATIONAL LIBRARY OF AUSTRALIA
A catalogue record for this book is available from the National Library of Australia

MIX
Paper | Supporting responsible forestry
FSC www.fsc.org FSC® C018684

ISBN 978 1 76 134697 2 (Paperback)

Penguin Random House Australia uses papers that are natural and recyclable products, made from wood grown in sustainable forests. The logging and manufacture processes are expected to conform to the environmental regulations of the country of origin.

penguin.com.au

We at Penguin Random House Australia acknowledge that Aboriginal and Torres Strait Islander peoples are the Traditional Custodians and the first storytellers of the lands on which we live and work. We honour Aboriginal and Torres Strait Islander peoples' continuous connection to Country, waters, skies and communities. We celebrate Aboriginal and Torres Strait Islander stories, traditions and living cultures; and we pay our respects to Elders past and present.